Coleen M. Paratore • *Illustrated by* Peter C

Catching the Sun

Charlesbridge

With love to Dylan, who taught me how to catch the sun
—C. M. P.

For Dr. Ted, who made every appointment with Chelsea a day at the beach
—P. C.

Published by Charlesbridge
85 Main Street
Watertown, MA 02472
(617) 926-0329
www.charlesbridge.com

Library of Congress Cataloging-in-Publication Data
Paratore, Coleen, 1958-
Catching the sun / Coleen M. Paratore; illustrated by Peter Catalanotto.
p. cm.
Summary: As Dylan and his mother enjoy being together at the beach early on his fifth birthday, he cannot help but think about the baby his mother will soon have, who will join them in this special time next summer.
ISBN 978-1-57091-720-2 (reinforced for library use)
[1. Mother and child—Fiction. 2. Beaches—Fiction. 3. Pregnancy—Fiction.
4. Sun—Rising and setting—Fiction. 5. Birthdays—Fiction.] I. Catalanotto, Peter, ill. II. Title.
PZ7.P2137 Cat 2008 [E]—dc22
2007001470

Printed in China
(hc) 10 9 8 7 6 5 4 3 2 1

Illustrations done in watercolor and gouache on illustration board
Display type and text type set in Calligraph 810 and Schneidler BT
Color separations by Chroma Graphics, Singapore
Printed and bound by Regent Publishing Services
Production supervision by Brian G. Walker
Designed by Diane M. Earley

The baby will be coming soon, but this morning, it's just me and Mom.

"Dylan," she whispers, and I jump up. We're going to catch the sun.

Dad is still honk-snoring away. Huck's in dog dreamland. His fur tickles as we sneak by.

"Happy birthday," Mom says.

"Thanks." I yawn, and Mom yawns back.

Outside it's dark and quiet. Two stars in the sky. Yesterday's sand crunches cold in my sneakers, but Mom's hand is warm.

We walk to the beach free as fish, no towels or toys to carry. I look up over Mom's mountain-belly and see the side of her smile.

Today's our last day on Cape Cod. My best week of the year: doughnuts and ice cream, riding the waves, biking to Clancy's for candy.

Mom likes the chowder and saltwater taffy, but her best thing is catching the sun. We do it every summer, just me and Mom. Next year, we'll have to bring the baby.

Mom says the sun always rises, but you can't always catch it. Sometimes it's cloudy, or you start watching a bird or a boat and you miss that first tiny blink of light.

After that the sun gets too big, and it would hurt your eyes to look.

Thursday was foggy. Yesterday we slept too late. Today is our last chance.

Close to the water, Mom stops to smell the beach roses. I always try to pick her some, but the thorns are sharp. I see clouds moving in. "Hurry, Mom."

At the beach stairs, the wind whooshes. The sky is purple now.

The ocean is breathing like a giant. *Ahhh . . . Shhhhh . . . Ahhh . . . Shhhhh. . . .*

We sit on the stairs. I lean on Mom's arm. "Watch the horizon," she says.

When I was born, Mom wrote me a song called "Dylan from the Sea." That's what my name means, *from the sea*.

When I was a baby, Mom rocked me to sleep singing that song.

When I was little, we bounced in these waves, singing my song together.

Now I'm big, and soon Mom will have a new baby to write a song for.

The clouds are growing. Where is the sun? "When will it come, Mom?"

"When it's ready." So we wait. Me and Mom and the sea.

A fish family skips across the waves. Sea gulls land—*caw, caw*—hunting up crabs for breakfast. Mom points to the sky. "Look."

I count the birds. "One, two, three, four . . . five."

"How did they know that's your number today?" Mom laughs and I laugh, too.

Now the sky is turning orange. "Like the start of a rainbow," I say.

Mom hugs her mountain-belly and smiles, probably thinking of the baby again.

I kick the railing hard.

Mom looks at me, then out to sea.

"I remember the day your dad and I sat here with a big book of baby names. When I read *Dylan*, I said, 'that's the one. My baby from the sea.' "

The sky is pink. The sun is coming. More clouds are coming, too. Hurry, sun, hurry. I want to jump or shout or something, but we sit quiet, waiting.

The sea breathes louder, *AHHH . . . SHHHHH . . . AHHH . . . SHHHHH. . . .*

“When it comes, look quickly,” Mom says, “then close your eyes.”

I stare at the horizon. Nothing. For a long time, nothing.

Then, like a birthday, without a sound, it comes.

A flash. A wink. A baby sun.

I shut my eyes. My heart's beating fast. Circles swirl in the dark in my head.

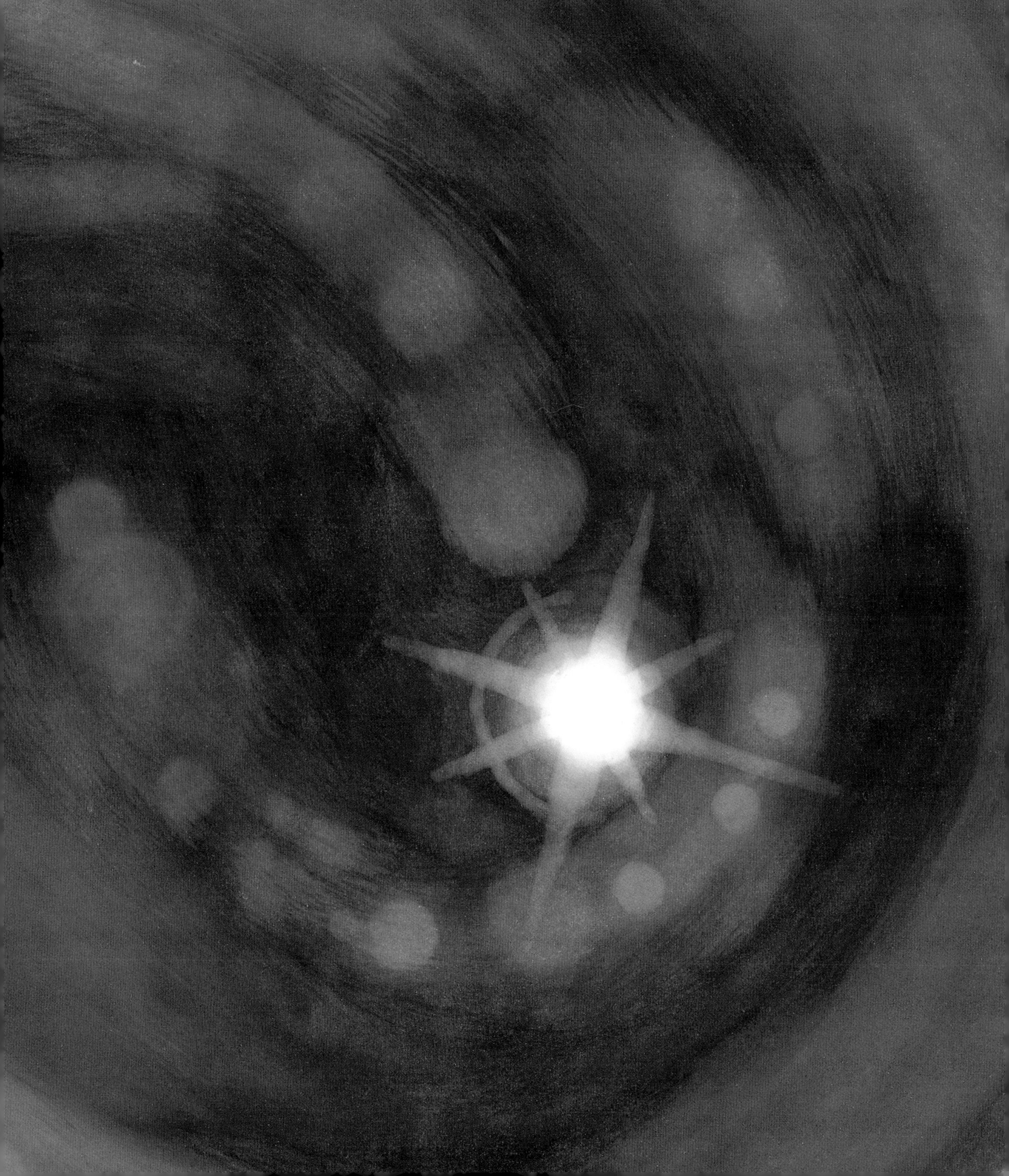

Then it clears and I see it. “I caught it, Mom. I caught the sun!”

Mom laughs. “I knew you would.”

I want to hug her, but I'm afraid if I move I'll lose the light.

Then, before I'm ready, it's gone.

"I lost it." I feel like crying.

"Dylan." Mom takes my face in her hands. "When you catch the sun with someone you love, it's a magic you never lose. Close your eyes and remember. It's all still there."

Later, crossing the bridge home, I wave goodbye to the waves.

We'll be back next year, and it will be fun, but it won't ever be the same. I start to feel bad, like I'm losing something. Then Mom turns around and looks at me.

She closes her eyes. She starts to smile. I close my eyes, too.

And there we are: just me and Mom, catching the sun on my birthday.